Disney Girls

Attack of the Beast

Gabrielle Charbonnet

NEW YORK

Printed in the United States of America.

First Edition

5   7   9   10   8   6   4

The text for this book is set in 15-point Adobe Garamond.

Library of Congress Catalog Card Number: 98-84797

ISBN: 0-7868-4160-5

For more Disney Press fun, visit www.DisneyBooks.com

Contents

Disney Girls

Attack of the Beast

Chapter One

My Day, My School, My Life

"*No!" the evil sorcerer screeched. He waved his enchanted . . .*"

His enchanted what? I wondered. Wand? Sword? His enchanted . . . lunch?

Lunch? I blinked. I was in my bedroom, sitting on my bed. I was holding an open book in one hand and my left shoe in the other.

"Isabelle, have you packed your lunch? Did you hear me?" my mother was calling from down the hall.

I glanced at the clock just as Mom walked through my open door. It was quarter to eight on Monday morning.

"Isabelle Beaumont!" she said, her eyes wide. "You're not even finished getting dressed? You're going to miss the bus! What have you been doing?" Then she saw the book in my hand.

She shook her head. "Never mind. I can tell. Put down that book, get dressed, and take two dollars from my purse for the school lunch. And hurry!"

"And then I missed the bus," I explained to my best friend, Jasmine Prentiss. Jasmine and I, and our friend Paula Pinto, were filing into our fourth-grade classroom at Orlando Elementary. Our teacher, Mr. Murchison, was straightening papers on his desk. He looked up and smiled as we came in. He's really nice, and he tries to pack excitement into learning ordinary things. So far I like him a lot.

"Did your mom give you a ride?" Paula asked.

"No." I made a face. "I had to catch a ride with the Beast."

Jasmine groaned and patted my shoulder. "I'm really sorry."

The Beast means Kenny McIlhenny—my next-door

neighbor. He's also in my class at Orlando Elementary. I call him the Beast because he's, well, beastly. There's no other way to put it.

"Maybe Mr. Murchison will give you some time before class so you can disinfect your clothes," Paula suggested.

"Ha ha," I said darkly.

My two friends broke up giggling. After a moment, I did, too.

"I have to admit," I said, "it was all my own fault. I got caught up in a really exciting chapter of *Once More the King*—you know, that fantasy series I'm reading? I just couldn't put it down, and the next thing I knew, Mom was throwing lunch money at me and pushing me out the door."

I sighed. This kind of thing happened to me pretty often. The problem was, I read *all the time*. Most people don't think reading is a problem. But I guess it can be if you do it practically every waking moment.

What can I say? I just love books—any book. I have favorite things to read: fantasy stories about wizards and dragons and magic. But I read other things, too: biographies (especially about women or girls), poetry, old-fashioned books, like *Little Women*, *A Secret Garden*, and *A Little Princess*. I even enjoy Nancy Drew and the Hardy Boys and The Three Investigators. The truth is, I'll read just about anything.

Once, in a doctor's waiting room, I ended up reading *Car and Driver* magazine. I read an entire article about carburetors. I thought it was interesting, too! I've read Mom's food magazines, Dad's copies of *Science Today*—you name it, I'll read it. And usually, it's fine. But sometimes, like this morning, it causes a problem.

Jasmine shook her head. "I don't know, girl. What are we going to do about you? You're more than a bookworm—you're a book anaconda. You devour them." Jasmine bared her teeth, trying to look like, I guess, an anaconda.

I laughed. "Well, books have always been my best friends—until now."

Jasmine smiled at me, and Paula laughed. Then Mr. Murchison said, "Ahem," and we all scrambled to sit down.

As Mr. Murchison began to call the roll, I let myself daydream a little bit. It was true: I had a real best friend now. Sometimes I still found it hard to believe. I've always had friends, but until I had met Jasmine just a month ago, I had never really had a *best* friend.

It's not like I'm an ogre or anything, and people can't stand me. That isn't it. But I've never really felt as if I fit in anywhere. I've always felt like an oddball. For one thing, I skipped second grade, because I was reading at a much higher level than my classmates. So I'm a year younger than anyone else in the fourth grade. And I'm short. So I look like I'm *two* years younger. That made it harder to make friends at my old school.

For another thing, I'm African-American. Here in Orlando, Florida, there are lots of other black people. My parents have a lot of black friends. But the neighborhood we live in is mostly white. My last school, the Janet Gregory School, was mostly white. At Orlando Elementary, it's about half white and half nonwhite (which means blacks and Asians and Native Americans). I'm more comfortable here.

The third thing that made me feel different is that I read all the time. I'd rather read than do almost anything else. I don't watch a lot of TV; I don't hang out at the mall; I don't stay on the phone all night. So when my friends at school talked about a show they watched, or a cute outfit at some store, I was always clueless. You got it—total oddball.

Then I transferred to Orlando Elementary. Guess what? I fit in here! And now, one month later, I have a really, truly *best* best friend, for the first time ever. Not only that, but I have four other best friends, too. Let me tell you how we all met. It's a great story.

Chapter Two

One Best Best Friend, Plus Four

You probably know by now that my name is Isabelle Beaumont. Actually, it's Isabelle Masika Beaumont. Masika is Swahili—it means "baby comes in the rain." My mom says it was pouring the day I was born.

I told you that I skipped second grade at my old school. They actually wanted me to skip two grades, but my parents said no. (I'm not a genius. In fact, math and science are a little hard for me. But my reading and vocabulary skills test really high, because I read so much. So teachers always think I'm super-smart.)

Even after skipping a grade, my parents felt my old school wasn't challenging me enough. Maybe it's because I read our whole reading textbook in one afternoon, and then I was bored the rest of the school year. Anyway, my parents decided to transfer me to Orlando Elementary, which is supposed to be harder academically.

I wasn't sure I wanted to change schools. Even though I didn't have any good friends at Janet Gregory, I was used to it. Also, Kenny McIlhenny went to OE, and I felt like I already saw enough of *him*. We live next door to each other in a suburb called Willow Hill. His parents and my parents are best friends. The idea of seeing Kenny all day, every day, didn't exactly thrill me.

But anyway, I started at OE on the second day of school. They put me into Kenny's class. Ugh. As if that wasn't bad enough, I could feel everyone looking at me, the new girl. I tried to pretend it didn't matter. I just sat at my desk wishing I was somewhere else.

Then it was lunchtime. It's one thing to act cool and collected during class. But to go to a strange cafeteria and eat by myself? I was dreading it. My stomach was tied up in knots. Then I realized I didn't even know where the cafeteria was. I almost wanted to cry.

I was wondering what on earth I would do when I noticed a girl smiling at me. She was short, like me, with long blond hair, green eyes, and a few freckles. With her was a taller girl with light-tan skin, dark brown hair just past her shoulders, warm brown eyes, and a friendly smile.

"Hi, I'm Jasmine Prentiss," said the blond girl. "Do you know where the cafeteria is?" It was like she'd read my mind!

"No, I don't," I said with relief. "Can I go with you?"

Jasmine and the other girl, whose name was Paula Pinto, showed me where the cafeteria was. Not only that, they asked me to sit with them at their usual table, with their three other friends.

I was surprised by how comfortable I was with Jasmine and Paula. And their friends—Ella, Yukiko, and Ariel— seemed great, too. At the time, I thought it was almost weird. Now I know that it was magic.

After that first day, Jasmine and Paula helped me feel at home at OE as much as they could—especially Jasmine. I was disappointed to find out that Jasmine lived way over in Wildwood Estates. Her family is really rich, and they live in a gigantic mansion. But the other girls all live in Willow Hill, like me.

Despite that, it was Jasmine whom I started to become real friends with. From the very beginning, we hit it off so well it was practically eerie. We laughed at the same jokes. We liked the same clothes. We even liked to read the same kinds of books! One afternoon we went shopping at the mall, and we both picked out the *exact same pair of sneakers.* We were made for each other!

For the first time in my life, I started to hope that I might actually have a best friend. I was both really happy and a little scared. I was scared because I had a big secret—and I thought if Jasmine ever found out about it, she would laugh at me.

The other thing that made me worry was the fact that Jasmine already had four other best friends. The five of them did everything together. Jasmine and Yukiko took ballet classes together. They all had parties and sleepovers at each other's houses. They all sat together at lunchtime every day. When we had mixed classes, for art or music or gym, they stuck to each other like Post-its. Why would she want *another* best friend?

They were all great, but somehow I felt like the odd girl out. When I told Jasmine how I felt, she brushed off my feelings and said everything was fine. But I could tell her friends were starting to wonder what was going on.

Then came that day at Walt Disney World. Our school had a field trip there to see an international dance troupe at Epcot. (I know: a field trip to Walt Disney World. I *love* living in Orlando!) Jasmine had asked me to be her field-trip buddy. Ella and Yukiko were paired up, and so were Ariel and Paula. The five of them were talking about good times they'd had, and I felt so alone. I offered to hang by myself, so I wouldn't ruin their day.

Instead, Jasmine insisted I come with her to Morocco. And there, in the little courtyard with a fountain, Jasmine changed my life. We looked into a mirror while she whispered:

All the magic powers that be,
Hear me now, my special plea.
Of worldly sights please set us free
And help us see what we should be.

11

Then, right in front of our eyes, we changed. Jasmine transformed from a blond, green-eyed fourth grader into dark-haired, dark-eyed Princess Jasmine, from the movie *Aladdin*. And I became, well, even more myself, if you know what I mean. I transformed into Belle, from *Beauty and the Beast*.

That was my secret. Outside, I might be ordinary Isabelle Beaumont. But inside I feel as if I'm really Belle, from my favorite movie. Everything she thinks and feels and does, I could think and feel and do. I just *am* her, in a way that's hard to explain. That was the biggest reason I always felt like an oddball.

And that was the reason Jasmine and I became *best* best friends—because she felt that way, too, about Princess Jasmine.

Now the really freaky part is when we got back together with Ella, Yukiko, Paula, and Ariel. I was still trying to absorb the fact that Jasmine was just like me in this special, secret way—and then it turned out that *all* of them were! They called themselves the Disney Girls, and each one of them had a magical connection to her favorite princess. Suddenly I could see it on their faces, as plain as anything. Ella was Cinderella, of course. Ariel was Ariel. Paula was Pocahontas. And Yukiko was Snow White.

For the first time in my life, I belonged somewhere. For the first time in my life, I could be *myself*. Suddenly I was part of a wonderful group, instead of being an outsider. I felt like a new person.

Since then the magic has only gotten stronger.

Chapter Three

Beaumont's

That afternoon I managed not to miss the school bus. Unlike my friends, who all go home after school, the bus usually drops me off at Beaumont's, which is the food shop my mom owns. Beaumont's is a really neat place. It has all sorts of fancy and weird foods, and wonderful things that you can't buy anywhere else in Orlando. Some items sound gross to me, like squid pickled in its own ink. But some things are fantastic, like kalamata olives or spicy shaved ginger or umeboshi plums.

(That's another thing Jasmine and I have in common—

we both like to try new foods. None of the other Disney Girls do.)

Usually I sit in my mom's office in the back and do my homework. But if I don't have much, or I finish early, then I help out a little in the store.

Sometimes I stock shelves, which means I replace foods that have been bought. Sometimes I straighten jars and packages and bottles, lining everything up. I enjoy it. Once Ariel came with me to Beaumont's after school. At first she thought it was cool, but she got bored pretty quickly. Ariel always likes to be running off to do something new.

What's really fun is when Jasmine comes to Beaumont's with me. We rush through our homework as fast as we can. Then we walk around the store, pretending we're in a far-off, exotic marketplace. Sometimes it's the marketplace from *Aladdin*. Sometimes it's the marketplace from Belle's little village. The two of us wander around, whispering to each other, pretending to examine wares and argue with shopkeepers. Jasmine acts as if she doesn't know she has to pay for things. Or I act as if everyone's looking at me, thinking I'm weird. It's great.

But today it was just me. I did my homework, then sorted through the imported Japanese pears. I took out all the ones that had scratches or bruises.

At last it was five o'clock. Mom and I said good-bye to everyone (the store stays open until nine o'clock). Then we headed out to the parking lot, where Mom's red Volvo station wagon was parked.

"Whew! What a day," said Mom, starting the car. "Sometimes it's really crazy in there. What about you? How was school?"

"Okay," I said. "The school lunch wasn't too bad. Music class was fun. And we're reading a play out loud for reading comprehension."

"That sounds interesting," Mom said.

"I just wish my friends and I could have every class together," I told her. "Instead of just art and music and gym. It's a drag that we're in different grades."

"But it's nice that you can have some time together every day," Mom pointed out. "Your old school didn't do that."

"Yeah, that's true," I agreed.

The thing is, Ella, Ariel, Yukiko, and I are all eight years old. The three of them are in third grade. Because I skipped a grade, I'm in fourth, with Paula and Jasmine. For some classes, OE puts several grades together, so we do get to see each other during the day. And we eat lunch together every day. In a perfect world, the six of us would be together all day long.

Suddenly I had a fantastic idea. I knew the Disney Girls had sleepovers pretty often. They took turns having them at each other's houses. But I had never hosted one.

"Mom," I said, "what are you doing this Saturday?"

My mother glanced at me. "Why do you ask?"

"Can I have a sleepover?" I asked in a rush. "It's really my turn, you know. The others have all had them, but I never have. If you're not doing anything special this Saturday, maybe I could have a sleepover, with all my friends."

I waited to hear what my mom would say. I had never hosted a sleepover in my life, because I had never had really good friends. I had only ever *been* to one sleepover, in third grade, and that was just because Sherry Lonstein's mom had made her invite every girl in the class. I hadn't liked it.

But I knew a sleepover with my five best friends would be completely different. I knew I wanted to have one more than anything. *Please, Mom, say yes*, I wished. I felt a tingle dancing along my arms, the way I did whenever magic was nearby.

"I think that sounds like fun," my mom said. "This Saturday should be fine. Ask your friends, and then we can decide on food and everything. Okay?"

"Okay!" I said happily. I beamed the whole way home. Everything was wonderful: school was great, I had four of the best friends I had ever hoped for, I had one extra-terrific best friend, *and* I was having my very first sleep-over—that is, if everyone could make it.

I was pretty sure they could. After all, magic was at work. . . .

Chapter Four

You Are Invited To . . .

By Wednesday everything was planned. I had not said one word about a sleepover to my friends. I wanted it to be a surprise, until I got everything ready. But I felt all keyed up—listening to hear if any of them had special weekend plans. What if one of them wanted to have a sleepover at her house, and asked everyone before I did?

I just kept wishing hard and trying to keep in touch with my magic. Have you noticed I've mentioned magic several times? That's because all of us, the Disney Girls, believe that magic is part of our everyday lives. It surrounds us, it helps us, it's in everything. All you have to do is look for it, and open yourself up to it, and there it is.

Before I saw *Beauty and the Beast*, I hadn't been that aware of magic. Then, when I saw myself moving across the theater screen, it was as if I had gotten a new prescription for glasses, and could suddenly see. Everything made more sense. I knew who I was. Then the Disney Girls showed me how magical everything is, and how special it is that we've found each other.

This week, all my sleepover wishing and hoping paid off. No one mentioned having special plans. No one asked me to a sleepover at her house. On Wednesday morning, Mom gave me a ride to school early. I didn't meet the DGs on the playground, as usual. Instead I sneaked around, putting invitations in all their cubbies.

When the bell rang, Paula and Jasmine rushed into our classroom with everyone else. I wished I could see Ariel's, Ella's, and Yukiko's faces when they opened their envelopes, but they were across the hall, in Ms. Timmons's third-grade class.

I sat at my desk, wound as tightly as a spring on one of my dad's inventions. (My dad really is an inventor. He works in the research and development department at a huge company. But he also invents things around the house in his spare time.) After Jasmine and Paula waved hello to me, they went to dump their books in their cubbies.

First Jasmine, then Paula found their envelopes. I had made all the invitations myself. The envelopes were purple, with each girl's name written on it in purple glitter ink. Inside was a white card. I used pink and gold glitter ink on the card to write:

You are invited to an evening of wonder, magic, and pizza.
Please come to a sleepover at Belle's cottage.
Saturday, 5:00
Disney Girls Only!

I thought they looked fantastic. But I had a last-minute case of the jitters. Would they all come?

I didn't have to worry. As soon as Jasmine finished reading hers, a huge smile made her whole face light up. She met my eyes and gave me a thumbs-up. Then I looked at

Paula. She looked happy and excited. From across the room, she nodded her head, and called, "I'll be there!"

Okay! Two down, three to go!

"Those were the coolest invitations, Isabelle," said Ella at lunchtime that day.

"You mean hottest," corrected Ariel. "If something is *totally* cool, then it's hot. Or maybe awesome. Or fab." She frowned in concentration and took a sip of chocolate milk.

Ella rolled her eyes. "*Whatever.* Anyway, Isabelle, I will definitely be there. I mean, as soon as I ask my dad. And my stepmom. But I bet they'll say yes."

Ella's dad recently remarried. Now Ella had a step-mother and two stepsisters, just like in *Cinderella*. Coincidence? I think not.

"I'll be there, too," said Ariel. "I have swim team practice at one o'clock, but it'll be over by three. Can I bring anything?"

Just like her namesake, Ariel is about as close to being a mermaid as you can get and still have legs. She's practically the star of OE's swim team, and she's only in third grade.

"No, thanks," I said happily. "Mom and I have everything planned."

"This is going to be so fun," said Yukiko. "I'll be happy to be away from the Dwarfs for one night. I might actually get some sleep."

Yukiko has *six* little brothers. Since she's Snow White, that makes them the Dwarfs. Here are two other interesting facts: her name, Yukiko, means *snow* in Japanese. And her mother was going to have another baby really soon—the *seventh* Dwarf! We were all wishing hard for a girl, but Yukiko was already prepared for another boy.

"Sleep?" I laughed. "Don't count on it. I have a lot of fun things planned. You probably won't even *want* to sleep."

"What? What do you have planned?" Jasmine asked eagerly.

I tried to look mysterious. "You'll see."

Chapter Five

Ready, Set, Go!

"Should we push the sofa against the wall?" I asked. "Or would it be better over here, by the TV?"

Jasmine squinted and pinched her lip. "By the wall," she decided. "We can still see the TV, but it'll give us plenty of room for our sleeping bags."

"Right," I said. "You're right." I trotted over to the basement stairs. "Dad!" I bellowed. "We need your help!"

I turned back to Jasmine. "I'm so glad you came over early to help me."

Jasmine grinned. "You don't really need help. You've done a great job of setting everything up." She paced the length of my family room. It takes up almost half our basement. We had decided to put our sleeping bags down here, since my bedroom is too small to hold all of us. Plus, the big TV is down here, and the VCR.

"Yes, this should be perfect," said Jasmine briskly. "If we put our sleeping bags in a half circle, we can still all see the TV, and have room to walk around, too."

"Okay," I said.

"What's up, girls?" asked my dad, coming downstairs.

"Can you help us move the sofa against the wall?" I asked. "We need more room here in the middle."

"All right," said my dad. He shifted the sofa for us. The family room suddenly seemed much bigger.

"Thanks, Dad," I said. "I'll call if we need you again."

Dad smiled at me and headed back upstairs.

"Now, we need to set up your CD player," Jasmine advised. "I brought over some CDs, but pick out some of your favorites, too. Do you have the *Beauty and the Beast* sound track?"

"Of course," I said. "I have all the sound tracks."

Jasmine grinned. "So do the rest of us. Let's put them by the CD player, so we'll be ready. And we can bring our sleeping bags down here and leave them rolled up."

Jasmine is just the best, best friend. She thinks of everything.

"Should I get all the stuff for the sundaes ready, up in the kitchen?" I asked.

Jasmine thought. "Nah," she said. "Plenty of time to do that after we get back from dinner. Now, what time is it?"

I glanced at my watch. "Oh, my gosh, it's four-thirty!" I cried. "They'll be here any minute!"

"Relax, relax," Jasmine said, laughing. "Everything's ready. You've planned a great sleepover. We'll have a blast. Just try to calm down."

"I can't help it!" I said. "It's my first sleepover. And why is my house so totally boring? I don't have a pool to swim in, like you; I don't have a fountain in my living room, like Yukiko."

"Your house is fine," said Jasmine firmly. "*You* are fine. You have a great family room and a great big backyard. Plus, you know the Disney Girls always have a fabulous time, whenever we're together. Quit worrying."

I swallowed hard. "You're right." I sat on the couch, try-ing to relax. But I couldn't. I was so nervous and excited about my first sleepover! I twirled one of my short braids and bit my lip.

Jasmine took one look at me and burst into laughter. "You're about as relaxed as a mouse at a python festival," she said. "Would it help if we made a special wish?"

"Yes!" I cried, leaping from the couch.

"Okay." Jasmine and I stood facing each other. We linked the pinkies on both hands. Very quietly we said:

All the magic powers that be,
Hear us now, our special plea,
This is Belle's first big test,
Please make her party a huge success.

Then we closed our eyes and wished. When I opened my eyes and looked into Jasmine's calm green gaze, I felt much, much better.

Ding, dong!

"They're here!" I shrieked.

Chapter Six

A Great Invention

Within ten minutes, my parents' little house was full of talking, laughing Disney Girls. Jasmine, Ariel, and Paula had been here before, but it was the first time I'd had Ella and Yukiko over.

"This is so nice," said Ella, looking around. "I like all of your parents' stuff."

I glanced around the living room, as if I was seeing everything for the first time. My parents *did* have some nice things, I guessed. My dad has traveled all over the world for his job, and he loves to bring home interesting

28

art and carvings and wall hangings—especially African ones.

"Are you guys ready to hit Little Ricky's Pizza Haven?" my mother asked as she walked into the living room.

"Yes!" we all cried.

My folks don't have a minivan, since they have only one child (me). So we had to take two cars to the pizza place. My dad drove Ella, Paula, and Ariel. My mom took me, Yukiko, and Jasmine. Just as we were all piling into the cars in our driveway, the Beast skateboarded by us, on his way home.

"Hi, Kenny," said my mom as she slid into the driver's seat.

"Hello, Mrs. Beaumont," Kenny sang sweetly. Then, when my mom closed her car door, he grinned at us. It was not a nice grin. "Oh, is it time for you all to head back to the funny farm?" he taunted. "It's nice they let you out once in a while." See what I mean about Kenny being beastly?

Ariel's eyes flashed, but I pushed her gently toward my dad's car. "Just ignore him," I said through clenched teeth. "Don't let him ruin our sleepover."

29

"Sleepover?" Kenny hooted. "Your parents are probably *paying* the Beaumonts to take you off their hands for one night."

I slammed the car door shut just as Ariel started to yell something back.

At Little Ricky's, my parents got a table for two, so the six of us could have our own booth. It was so great—we ordered for ourselves and everything. (We got a large half pepperoni-and-mushroom and half vegetarian pizza with extra cheese. It was fantastic.)

After the pizza, we piled back into our two cars and headed home again. Mom and I had gotten all the ingredients to make homemade sundaes. I was looking forward to piling tons of fudge sauce and whipped cream and nuts on mine.

But when we got home, my dad had a surprise for us. As we gathered around the kitchen table, he pulled out a large, bulky object covered with an old sheet.

"What in the world is that?" I asked.

Dad whipped off the sheet. "Ta-daaaa!" he said proudly.

It looked like a cross between a can opener and a car wreck.

Dad looked at our blank faces. "It's a sundae-making machine!" he said. "Obviously. I've been working on it for days."

"Ohhh," I said. "Now I see. Well, let's try it out. Everyone grab a bowl."

That's my dad—Mr. Inventor. A lot of times his inventions are great—like the pulley system inside the garage that hoists groceries right from the car up to the kitchen. But sometimes he creates something that, frankly, needs more work. As my friends lined up eagerly with their bowls and spoons, I hoped Dad had worked all the kinks out of this latest invention.

"Okay, Yukiko—you be the first victim," Dad joked. "Place your bowl on the *X*." He had made a small *X* on the kitchen table with some masking tape. Yukiko put her bowl right on top of it.

At first, the sundae-maker worked great. Dad put a carton of ice cream on the table and turned on the machine. A mechanical arm whirred to life and swung over to the ice cream. A built-in scoop rolled up a nice ball of ice cream and dropped it neatly in Yukiko's bowl. My friends oohed and aahed.

"Strawberry, butterscotch, or chocolate sauce?" my dad asked, pressing buttons on a remote control.

"Strawberry," said Yukiko.

A small tube stuck out from the side of the machine and dolloped a big serving of sauce right on top of the ice cream. Whipped cream, nuts, and a cherry followed. The sundae was absolutely perfect.

"Voila!" my dad said, smiling happily.

"Yay!" we all said, clapping.

Jasmine stepped up and quickly placed her bowl on the X. Just as before, the machine scooped up ice cream, plopped it in the dish, ladled on sauce (Jasmine wanted fudge), squirted whipped cream, and sprinkled on nuts.

"All right!" Jasmine said, taking her bowl. "I'm impressed."

I grinned at my friends. So far, so good, with my first sleepover.

"My turn!" Ella put her bowl on the X.

The sundae-maker scooped up ice cream, swung over, and plopped the ice cream neatly . . . on the table outside of Ella's bowl.

"Oops," said Dad. He pressed some buttons on the

remote. The second scoop of ice cream landed in the bowl. However, Ella's butterscotch sauce got ladled onto the kitchen floor. Dad was pressing buttons as fast as he could. Then . . .

Squirt! The machine squirted whipped cream right in Ella's face! Next it pelted Ariel with chopped nuts!

"Ow! Ow!" Ariel said, trying to protect herself from the flying nuts.

"Turn it off, Dad!" I cried, waving my arms. "Turn it off!"

Chapter Seven

Coming to You Live

"Are you okay?" I asked Ella as she washed the whipped cream off her face.

Ella giggled. "I'm fine. Actually, it was kind of fun. Like being at a carnival or something. The pie-throwing contest."

I was relieved Ella was taking it so well. It wasn't Dad's fault, exactly, but I was pretty embarrassed. The rest of us finished making our sundaes by hand. Dad took his invention down to his basement workshop, muttering, "If I realign the final gear . . ."

Anyway. Once Ella was cleaned up, we took our sundaes down into the family room. I made sure Ariel hadn't been blinded by rocketing pieces of chopped nuts.

"No big deal," she insisted. "Stuff happens."

"Yeah, especially when my dad is around," I said, but I couldn't help smiling. The look on Ella's face when she got squirted with whipped cream *was* pretty funny—even if I never wanted it to happen again.

The next thing I knew, we were all laughing. I had to lean over on the couch and pound one of the pillows, I was laughing so hard. Ariel stood up and pretended to be dodging chopped nuts again. She held her hands in front of her face and leaned this way and that.

"Ow!" she said, giggling. "Ow! Please! No more nuts. I'll tell you what you want to know!"

Our neighbors down the block could probably hear us, howling with laughter.

Eventually we calmed down. I was so happy, being with my friends, laughing and talking and having a good time.

"Are you guys almost ready for our film festival?" I asked.

"Yeah!" Jasmine said. "What should we watch?"

Jasmine had already told me that the DGs always watch at least one movie, and sometimes two or three at their sleepovers.

"We can do eeny, meeny, miney, mo," I said, getting up. "But first, let me ask my mom for some popcorn." I ran upstairs, and Mom helped me fix a gigantic bowl of popcorn and some sodas. When I got back downstairs, Jasmine had put on the CD from *Beauty and the Beast*.

I put the popcorn on the table and handed out the sodas. Without realizing it, I hummed along with Belle's song, and even sang under my breath.

"Gee, you have a nice voice," said Yukiko. "You sound a lot like Belle."

I was pleased to hear it. I had sung along with that song so many times, and I tried hard to make my voice blend with Belle's.

"I have this CD of Sing-Along songs," said Jasmine, holding it up. "It has all our themes on it." She put it in the CD player and turned it on.

Then the sleepover really took off. Ella, Ariel, and I changed into our nightgowns. We all grabbed our hairbrushes, my dad's golf clubs, anything that looked like a microphone. Each one of us sang our own personal theme song, as loud as we could.

I had even worked out a little routine with mine, where I walk along, swinging a basket, just like Belle did in the movie. I knew exactly where to stop and turn around, and how to look as if I was running up a pretty hill covered with flowers. I put all my heart into it, and belted out the song I knew so well, about how I wanted much more than this provincial life.

My friends clapped and whistled when I was done. Then the rest of them took turns, singing and acting out their songs. I could hardly believe how good everyone was. I guess I wasn't the only one who had practiced a million times. And you know what? When each girl was singing, she actually started to look more like her character. (Later, Jasmine said the same thing had happened to me.)

In between the theme songs, we acted out the crowd scenes and some of the other songs from the movies. Since we all knew every word by heart, it was easy. And it was so, so much fun.

For "Be Our Guest," we danced in a circle and

pretended to fall over, just like the spoons did in the movie. For "Kiss the Girl," we pretended to be different kinds of fish and crabs and frogs and clams, all singing. For the mice's song in *Cinderella*, we danced around, singing in high, squeaky voices.

It was just about the most fun I'd ever had in my entire life.

The six of us were clapping as we heard the intro music to "Circle of Life," when suddenly we heard a sharp *thump!* against one of the basement windows.

I stopped in my tracks. "What was that?" I peered at the window, but I couldn't see anything. "Was that a raccoon or something?"

Then I had a very bad thought: the Beast lives right next door. And he had seen us all together earlier.

"Oh, my gosh," I wailed, putting my hands on my cheeks. "Kenny McIlhenny!"

Chapter Eight

Mark of the Beast

Before I had even finished saying his name, Ariel and Paula had raced to the basement door and flung it open. (In Florida, basements are not actually dug into the ground. So even though our basement is below our house, we didn't have to climb up steps to get out of it.)

Paula and Ariel tore into the backyard, and the rest of us pounded after them.

At first our yard looked totally normal. Then we all saw it: a dark figure slithering over the wooden fence into the McIlhennys' backyard. And what was dangling from one hand? A video camera!

"It's him!" I cried. "Let's get him!"

I started to run to the fence, but Paula stopped me. "Wait a second," she said. "Let's think this thing through." How could Paula be so calm in the middle of this emergency?

"What's to think about? Let's get him!" I said.

"Hang on, hang on," said Paula. "What happens if we run over there? His parents will be pretty surprised. He'll pretend we're imagining everything. He'll look like the victim. And *your* parents will be upset that we left the house without telling them. We don't even have any proof that he did anything, after all. Let's go back inside and think about what to do."

That's Paula: levelheaded.

"Okay," I said reluctantly. "I guess you're right."

On our way back inside, we stopped in front of the window where we'd heard the sound. Sure enough, right in my dad's flower bed were the marks of two sneakers. That little stinker *had* been peeping in through our window! While we were dancing and singing and goofing around! I groaned and stomped my foot.

We trooped back inside. I switched off the music and closed all the window blinds. The six of us sat around glumly, looking at each other.

"Isn't being a Peeping Tom illegal?" I asked. "Maybe we should call the police." I was getting angrier and angrier the more I thought about it.

"His parents are your parents' best friends," Jasmine pointed out. "His parents would be pretty upset if you called the police. They might get mad at your parents. Then your parents might get mad at you."

"Why would they get mad at me?" I demanded, holding out my arms. "*He's* the Peeping Tom!"

"He's not a real Peeping Tom," said Paula. "He's just a fourth grader being a jerk."

"And that's not illegal," said Ella.

"Even though it should be," said Yukiko.

Now I was really steaming. My parents and the McIlhennys had lived next door to each other since before Kenny and I were born. Kenny had been a rock in my shoe for as long as I could remember. He had thrown sand at me when we were toddlers. He had pretended to eat a frog and made me cry when we were in kindergarten. He had thrown water balloons at me every summer, my whole life. He had leaped out of bushes at me, made prank phone calls, and wrote "Isabelle is a total sissy" on our wooden fence with chalk. Throughout everything, I had tried to ignore him, and all the dumb things he did, so I wouldn't upset my parents.

But now he had gone too far.

"Guys," I said grimly. "The Beast spied on us. He's ruined our sleepover. And he probably videotaped us doing secret Disney Girl things. I think you all know what this means."

One by one I met my friends' eyes. Ella and Yukiko seemed timid and a little fearful. Paula was curious. Ariel had a look of outrage on her face. Jasmine waited for me to finish.

"This means war," I said.

Chapter Nine

Magic, Where Are You?

Thanks to the Beast, the rest of the sleepover was not as fun as I had planned. Although we had closed every single blind on every single window, we still felt self-conscious. We ate our popcorn and watched *The Parent Trap* and *Snow White*, but I could tell my friends were all upset about what had happened.

The next morning, Mom made waffles with fresh strawberries and maple syrup. They were delicious, but I could hardly eat.

"Don't worry, it wasn't your fault," Jasmine told me, right before everyone left on Sunday.

I hung my head miserably. "I should have known," I moaned. "Why didn't I close the blinds earlier? I've lived next door to Kenny my whole life. Why didn't I suspect something?"

"You can't plan for every disaster," said Ella kindly.

"In a way, it's a good thing," Paula said. "Now we know to expect the worst from him. We'll be on guard." Paula always tries to see the bright side of things. But there was no bright side of this.

I waved good-bye to my friends sadly. After they had gone, I shuffled into my room and flopped into my beanbag chair.

"What's the matter, honey?" my mom asked, coming into my room. "You look terrible."

"Thanks," I sighed. I had been waiting for my friends to leave before I told my mom about the Kenny problem. I was sure I would tell her—I usually tell her everything. (Not about being Belle, but almost everything else in my life.)

But right this minute, I suddenly decided not to tell

44

her—at least for a while. I knew that if I told her, she would take my side. She would probably insist on telling Kenny's parents, so they could punish him. (That's what she did when he led an enormous colony of ants into my wading pool by dribbling a line of honey across our lawn. That was back when we were both six.)

To tell you the truth, I didn't feel like dragging my parents into it. I wanted to handle this disaster by myself—at least for a while. I especially didn't want Kenny to say, "Oh, this tape? Gee, I don't remember what's on it. Why don't we all watch it together, okay, Mom? Okay, Mrs. Beaumont? Can you see all right from where you're sitting, Dad?"

Kenny the Beast McIlhenny is *totally* capable of doing something that awful. That low.

I didn't know if I could live through something like that.

So now I managed a smile for my mom. "Oh, I'm okay," I told her. "I guess I'm just tired. We probably stayed up too late last night, talking." I blinked and tried to look innocent. (This is when having big brown eyes comes in handy.)

Mom smiled at me and tugged one of my braids. "Well, that's what sleepovers are all about," she said. Then she left my room, humming.

All day Sunday I moped around. I tidied up the family room downstairs, gritting my teeth at the awful memory of seeing Kenny slithering over the fence. Dad helped me put the couch back in position. I vacuumed up little bits of popcorn off the floor. Then I carried my sleeping bag upstairs and shoved it to the back of my closet.

Mostly, I just felt bad all day. It had been the very first sleepover I had ever had. I had planned every detail. Thought up all sorts of fun things to do. Tried to have everything perfect.

And look what had happened: Kenny had ruined everything.

After lunch I sat at my desk and wrote down a list of ways to get even with Kenny.

1. Tell him he smells bad. (He would probably be happy.)
2. Hide his schoolbooks. (He probably wouldn't mind.)

3. Put gum on his chair at school. (He'd see it for sure.)
4. Put paste in his hair. (Teacher would see me.)
5. Make up something awful about him and tell everyone. (I just didn't think I could this.)

Finally I gave up. At least I had my five best friends working on the problem, too. That is, if they still *were* my friends. Just then, Jasmine called.

I picked up the phone. "Hello?"

"Hi," said Jasmine. "I bet you're sitting around, stewing about the Beast, right?"

I smiled into the phone. "Yeah," I admitted.

"Look, between the six of us, we'll come up with something, okay?" said Jasmine. "You're not in this alone. And remember, it was not your fault."

For the first time all day I felt like I could breathe. "Okay," I said. "Thanks."

"See you tomorrow," she said, and hung up.

Isn't she a great friend?

Right before dinner, I tried to make a special magic wish to help me know what to do. But I couldn't concentrate. The magic wasn't there. I guess I was still too angry and upset. Jasmine says that your mind has to be clear and happy for the magic to work best. That ruled me out.

The only thing that made me feel better was to curl up in my beanbag with my latest book. In *Once More the King*, Prince Drigannon had just entered the dragon's cave. I stayed glued to it till dinnertime.

"Did you feed Snuffles and Pokey tonight?" my dad asked as I was sitting down to a nice plate of linguine with white clam sauce. Snuffles and Pokey are our two dogs. They're just mutts, but they're good pets. Before I knew the Disney Girls, they were my best friends. My parents and I take turns feeding them, brushing them, and taking them for walks.

"Oops, no, I forgot," I said, twirling some linguine around my fork. Dad reached over and lowered my fork to my plate.

"You may eat your dinner after you feed the dogs," he said firmly.

"But it will be cold by the time I get back," I protested. "Clam sauce is yucky when it's cold. Can't the dogs wait?"

My mom frowned. "That's the second time this week you've forgotten to feed Snuffles and Pokey. They're just animals—they can't open their own cans of dog food. It's our responsibility to feed them."

I got up and stomped into the kitchen, mostly so I wouldn't have to listen to the rest of the lecture. I felt bad when I saw Pokey waiting patiently by his dish, and Snuffles looking at me accusingly with her big doggy eyes.

"I'm sorry," I muttered as I opened a can of dog food and split it between their bowls. "I forgot." I gave them fresh water and refilled the kibble dish they share. Then I marked off my space on the chore chart and went back to the dining room. Mom handed me my plate and I microwaved it for forty seconds.

I sighed. What a day.

The week didn't begin any better, either. I stayed up late reading *Once More the King* under my covers with my flashlight, so I could hardly open my eyes on Monday morning. I had to rush to get ready for school so I wouldn't miss the bus again. There was no way I would risk having to ride with Mrs. McIlhenny and the Beast.

At school I realized I had left my spelling book at home—with my homework in it. Spelling is one of my all-time best subjects, so I was doubly mad that I couldn't hand it in.

The final straw was when I was putting my books in my desk. I felt something rumple up inside, so I reached in and pulled it out. It was a note on a plain white piece of paper. Someone had cut letters out of newspapers and magazines to create a message:

I HaVe THE tapE. AwaIT my DEmands.

I gnashed my teeth together so hard it hurt. I crumpled the paper and shoved it to the back of my desk.

Just then, someone behind me started humming. It took only a split second for me to recognize the tune to Belle's theme song. I whirled. Kenny! He was humming the tune, staring straight at me. So he *had* captured us on film, performing our theme songs!

I turned to look at Paula and Jasmine. They were glaring at Kenny, too. Then they met my eyes. Paula looked very solemn. Jasmine looked furious! And I felt just terrible.

Chapter Ten

Don't Get Mad, Get Even

Guess what. It got worse.

That day, I seriously considered going through Kenny's backpack. Maybe he had brought the tape with him to school. His backpack was hanging in his cubby. Did I have what it takes to actually go through someone else's stuff?

The answer is . . . no. I just couldn't, no matter how much I wanted to.

In science class, Kenny and I ended up next to each other as Mr. Murchison was handing out dishes to grow

51

carrot tops in. I was totally and completely ignoring the Beast.

He, however, was not ignoring me. Instead, he started humming the theme song to *America's Most Humiliating Home Videos*. For a few moments, I didn't make the connection. All I thought was, Kenny sure does like to hum theme songs.

Then it hit me: *America's Most Humiliating Home Videos!*

Oh, no! As soon as Kenny saw my expression, he looked smug.

I turned away. I was not about to give the Beast the satisfaction of seeing me upset. On the other hand, I *was* upset. Kenny was trying to tell me that he was planning on sending the tape to that show on TV. If he did, millions of people would watch me, Ariel, Yukiko, Paula, Jasmine, and Ella acting pretty silly.

How would we ever go to school again?

How would we ever go out in public again?

The worst thing was, what if being publicly humiliated changed how we felt about being Disney Girls? Right now, being a Disney Girl was a dream come true for me—and for all the others, too. It was part of who we were, and it made us happy. But what if everyone laughed at us because they didn't understand? I almost moaned out loud.

I decided to keep Kenny's note a secret. I didn't want the other DGs to worry, or to be as upset as I was. And I guess I was still hoping for a miracle—or some magic.

On Tuesday, I found another note in my desk. It said:

WhAt aRe You bRingIng FOR shoW 'n' TelL? I knOw whAt i'm BRinGiNg! SeE yOu tHuRsDaY. (EveRyOnE WilL.)

Again, I crumpled the paper and shoved it to the back of my desk. I have never been so angry in my entire life. Usually, it takes a lot to get me really angry. I tend to be pretty calm and even-tempered, and I don't like to hurt anyone's feelings. I try to be nice to everybody. But Kenny has always been able to get under my skin. He knows just how to push my buttons, and the next thing I know, I'm yelling at the top of my lungs.

I hate that.

Now Kenny was threatening to show the tape during

53

class on Thursday. People had shown videos in class before—Alan Hill had shown us a video of him catching a big fish. Allison Mason had shown us a tape of her family's booth at a craft fair. But no one had ever seen a tape of the Disney Girls singing and dancing in their pajamas.

I couldn't keep this to myself any longer. I had to tell the others. One by one, throughout the day, I slipped each of my five friends a note:

Emergency meeting of the DGs. My house, after school. Urgent!—Belle.

"Thanks for coming," I said later that afternoon. The six of us were crowded into my room. Ariel, Ella, and Yukiko were sitting on my bed. Jasmine was sunk down in my beanbag chair. Paula sat at my desk. I was standing in front of my closet. Before we had started the meeting, Mom had helped us make a big bowl of popcorn. Now we were taking turns digging into it.

"I guess we could have had the meeting at Beaumont's," Jasmine teased me. "Right between the cheese case and the vegetable section."

We all giggled. Then I got serious. Reaching past Paula, I took Kenny's two notes out of my backpack. Silently, I passed them around. One at a time, my friends read them. I saw their eyes grow round, and anger and disbelief cross their faces.

"Isabelle!" Jasmine exclaimed. "How could you keep these to yourself? You should have told us right away."

"You don't have to handle this alone," said Paula. "We're in this together."

"That's right," said Ella. "Kenny is such a fink!"

"I know, I know," I said. "But what can we do?"

Just then my mom tapped on my door. "Isabelle?"

I opened it and stuck my head out. "Yes?"

"Did Aunt Lina call yesterday?" Mom asked.

"Oops!" I smacked my palm against my forehead. "I'm sorry, Mom, I forgot to tell you. She called yesterday afternoon."

Mom looked irritated. "Well, because you didn't tell me, I didn't call her back. Now she thinks I didn't call her back on purpose, and she's annoyed with me. You need to be more responsible. Now I have to go straighten out this misunderstanding with her."

I went back in my room. Ugh. I had messed up again. I had been in the middle of an argument between two wizards in *Once More the King* when the phone had rung. I would have to apologize to Aunt Lina. But right now I had to put that problem aside so I could concentrate on stopping the Beast.

"I think I know what we should do," said Paula. "I've been thinking and thinking, and this plan just might work."

"What, what?" I asked eagerly. We all leaned forward.

Chapter Eleven

The Magic Mirror

The very next afternoon we put Paula's plan into action. To tell you the truth, I didn't think it would work. But it was the only plan anyone had come up with, so we had to try.

All of us except Jasmine waited for Kenny by the school buses. (Jasmine gets picked up every day by her mother, or her mother's driver. School buses make her mom nervous.)

"Let me know what happens, guys," Jasmine reminded us as she headed to her car.

"I'll call you tonight," I promised.

Anyway, we stood there, waiting for Kenny. Finally he came out of school with some of his friends—Alan Hill, Eric Morgenstein, and Rob Taglieri.

Ariel stepped forward. "Kenny, we need to talk to you," she said, her hands on her hips.

Alan stopped and grinned at Kenny. "Ooh, Kenny, they need to talk to you," he said in a singsong voice.

"Maybe they want to know when you're going shopping together," Rob teased him.

"Can you come to my tea party?" Eric asked in a high squeaky voice.

Inside, I groaned. Now Kenny would *really* be mad at us.

I glanced at him. Yep. He looked furious.

"I don't need to talk to *you*," he snapped.

But Paula and Yukiko stood in front of him. They're both pretty tall. He stopped, scowling. Still snickering, his friends got on the school bus. They peered out the windows at us.

"Listen, Kenny," Paula said in a calm voice. "We need to talk to you about the videotape. We know you don't really plan to do anything mean with it. You just wanted to tease us." Paula smiled and held out her hands. "Okay, you've teased us. We admit it: you got us. You won. It was funny, but now it's over. Show us you're really a nice guy by giving us the tape. Okay?"

That had been Paula's big plan. She thought we should talk to Kenny, reason with him. Maybe if we admitted that he had gotten the better of us, he would hand the tape back, no problem.

I agreed it was worth a shot, but I didn't think we'd be able to reason with the Beast. Paula doesn't know Kenny like I do.

Kenny stared at Paula in disbelief. Then he laughed.

"You've got to be kidding!" he hooted. "Do I look like a total sap? Get real. The tape is mine. You're just going to have to wait for me to think up the best thing to do with it."

As we watched in silent dismay, he brushed past us and joined his friends on the school bus to Willow Hill.

I sighed and rubbed my forehead. "Okay. Now on to plan B. Whatever it is."

*   *   *

Kenny kept us hanging Thursday, Friday, Saturday, and Sunday. You can imagine what total wrecks we were, waiting for the ax to fall. Would he show the tape at Show and Tell? He didn't. Would it appear on Friday night's edition of *America's Most Humiliating Home Videos*? It didn't.

And while we waited, we tried to think of a new plan. But the six of us just couldn't agree on what to do.

"I say we storm his house," Ariel said on Sunday morning. We had all met at Willow Green, which is the small park in Willow Hill. For a while we had skated around, but now we were resting on a long bench, and eating snowballs.

Ariel licked her snowball, her face set in a dark frown. "Just push past him, run through the house, and take his room apart till we find the tape."

"We can't do that," Jasmine said glumly. "Though it would be fun." She slurped up some juice from the bottom of her cup.

"Maybe we could drop down on him," Ariel suggested. "From a tree. Then we could tie him up—"

"Ariel," said Paula patiently.

"Every day I sit in class and worry," said Ella. "Kenny's

friends with Rob Taglieri, who's in our class. Sometimes I think Rob's smirking at me."

"Maybe he likes you," said Yukiko.

"Oh, please," Ella groaned. "Of course not. He's a *boy*. But what if Kenny showed him the tape?"

"I still say we should tell his parents," said Jasmine. "It was a horrible thing he did. He should be punished."

"We don't have any firm proof," I reminded her. "You know the worst thing, guys? I haven't felt any magic in my life since this happened."

We looked at each other uncertainly.

"It's because I've been too angry and upset," I went on sadly. "The magic won't flow when I feel like this. I have to do something. I just don't know what."

We went all day Monday without having any new ideas, and without Kenny giving us any more clues. I tried to ignore him, but it was as if I had a black rain cloud hanging over my head. Every time I looked at Kenny, all I saw was a beast—complete with claws, fangs, and rough brown fur.

When the three o'clock bell rang, I slowly began

gathering the books I would need for homework that night.

"I'll see you outside," said Jasmine, and Paula nodded.

"I'll be right out," I said dully.

"Oh, Kenny?" said Mr. Murchison. "May I see you for a moment?"

I froze. Was this it? Had Kenny asked to show the tape at Show and Tell? Maybe Mr. Murchison was giving him permission. I closed my backpack and stood up, watching Kenny curiously as I walked out of the classroom.

Outside in the hall, the school seemed empty and silent. I had dawdled so long that just about everyone had left.

A tingle went up my spine, and an idea hit me. Tiny prickles of electricity tickled the ends of my fingers. I realized a little bit of magic had come back! And I suddenly knew what I had to do.

Chapter Twelve

Taming the Beast

In my backpack, I keep a small hand mirror, no bigger than my palm. It's come in handy several times. Now I leaned against the wall outside our classroom, cleared my mind, and gazed deeply into the mirror.

All the magic powers that be,
Hear me now, my special plea.
The Beast is right behind this door—
Please show me what he has in store.

The image of my face cleared, and I could see Mr. Murchison standing at his desk. Next to him stood a small beast, looking glum, his fangs shiny and white.

"I'm sorry to tell you this, Kenny," said Mr. Murchison. "But you're falling way behind in reading. Your last two test scores have been well below average."

The Beast's horns seem to droop on either side of his ears.

"And it's clear you haven't been doing all of the homework," continued Mr. Murchison gently.

In the mirror, now glowing with magic, I saw the Beast slowly transform from a hideous, ugly animal into an embarrassed, unsure fourth grader: Kenny. His head was hanging down, and his cheeks were bright red.

"I'm afraid if you perform badly on the next test, two weeks from now, I'll have no choice but to put you in a remedial reading group."

"I understand," Kenny mumbled.

"Please let me know if I can help," said Mr. Murchison.

Kenny muttered something I couldn't hear, then shuffled toward the door, his head low.

As quick as a blink, I shoved the mirror into my backpack and skibbled silently down the hall as fast as I could.

I was already hatching a plan.

That afternoon I asked Mom to take me home early from Beaumont's. Then I hung around my bedroom window, waiting for the right moment. It didn't take too long: soon Kenny came out into his backyard with his dog, Otto.

"Here, Otto," Kenny said. "Catch, boy!" He threw a ragged lime-green tennis ball, and Otto barked happily and raced to catch it.

I ran downstairs, out our backdoor, and across our yard. Then I shimmied up our sweet olive tree, the one that hangs over a little bit into the McIlhennys' yard.

Kenny still looked glum, but he was throwing the ball gamely over and over for Otto.

"Oh, Kennnnyy," I sang, waving my hand. He looked up, saw me, and scowled.

I slithered out onto a branch and dropped neatly into his yard. His eyes narrowed. Then he launched into an incredibly lame rendition of "Be Our Guest."

It didn't bother me. "I have a confession," I said calmly.

That got his attention, and he shut up.

So I let it all come out—how I had "accidentally" eavesdropped that afternoon at school, and how I knew he was having serious trouble in reading.

"That's none of your business, Miss Nosy!" he said angrily, starting to walk inside.

"Just like our sleepover wasn't any of *your* business, Mr. Nosy?" I snapped back. "That didn't stop *you.*"

Kenny stopped and turned around again. "So what do you want?" he growled, sounding beastly.

"I want the tape," I said.

"Ha! Forget it," he said. He crossed his arms over his chest.

"No, I don't think I'll forget it," I said innocently, looking up at the sky. "Just like I won't forget that you might be put into a remedial reading class. Or that Mr. Murchison might even want to put you back in third grade."

I had no reason to think this. But I wanted to torture Kenny a little bit, to even things up. I try to be a good person as much as I can, but Kenny has a way of bringing out the worst in me.

66

Now his eyes got round. He hadn't thought of that. He looked horrified.

"But that wouldn't be so bad," I said kindly. "You and Rob Taglieri would be in the same class. It might even be fun."

The Beast looked like he was about to keel over.

"Of course," I continued, leaning against their fence, "I guess Eric Morgenstein might think it was kind of funny. Especially since he was last year's spelling bee champion. I'd sure hate to have to tell him about it. Him—and everyone else at school."

The Beast looked very pale. I was enjoying myself.

"What do you want, you fiend?" Kenny whispered.

Time to get down to business. "Well, Kenny," I said briskly, "I myself happen to be a great reader. I can read practically anything. And I'm willing, this one time, to help you catch up in our class. I could go over past lessons, coach you on the homework, and help you prepare for our next test."

His eyes narrowed again. "Why would you be willing—oh."

"Bingo. I want that tape," I said. "Plus I want a written

note from you saying that you promise never to tell anyone about it. If you get a C or above on the test, you have to give it to me. Do we have a deal?"

It wasn't a difficult question, but it was killing the Beast. The humiliating tape was the best thing he'd ever had on me. But we both knew he didn't really have a choice.

"You have to promise you'll never tell anyone about this," Kenny said in a last show of bravery.

"Deal," I said.

Reluctantly he stepped forward and we shook hands.

"Come over after dinner," I said, turning to climb back over the fence. "We'll get started tonight."

Chapter Thirteen

The Secret Lessons

On Tuesday at lunchtime, Ariel waved Jasmine, Paula, and me over to our usual table.

"I have it!" she said excitedly, ripping open a bag of chips. "We dress up in disguise, and wait outside Kenny's house till we're sure he isn't there. Then we ring the doorbell and tell his mother that we're from a video store. We say her son may have rented a video with a serious problem. We need to look at all their videos. Then we find the right one, say we have to take it back to the office to fix it, and leave." She beamed at us. "Brilliant, huh?"

"That's pretty good," said Ella, taking her sandwich out of her lunch bag. "Do you think his mom would go for it?"

"Um, somehow I don't think so," I said gently. I put my straw into my milk carton. "But you know, guys, I don't think we have to worry about the Beast anymore. I looked into my magic mirror last night, and it showed me that Kenny is probably just going to forget all about the tape."

Five friends stared at me.

"What?" Jasmine squealed.

I shrugged casually. "Just trust me. I think the whole tape thing is a closed book. So to speak."

Of course the other Disney Girls didn't buy it so easily. I was dying to tell them the truth, but I was sworn to secrecy.

That whole week at school, Kenny seemed a little down. He didn't tease us or talk to us or anything. My friends were very suspicious, but I didn't let on what I knew.

One time when Kenny was waiting impatiently for Paula to finish drinking at the water fountain, he started humming "Hakuna Matata." But one look from me shut him up.

"What is going *on*?" Ariel demanded after Kenny had slunk away.

I shrugged innocently. "I guess Belle has the magical power to tame the Beast."

Paula looked like she was going to die of curiosity, but she didn't press me for details.

"Okay, now," I told Kenny on Thursday afternoon. "This book is about American patriots during the Revolutionary War. I got it from the library because I thought you might like it."

Kenny yawned hugely and pretended to fall asleep.

I had expected this. I was prepared. "Look. This first story is about a field doctor who treated soldiers during the war. Sometimes he had to saw off their legs without giving them any anesthetic."

Kenny sat up straighter and looked over at the book.

"This story is about a spy who ran messages back and forth between different generals. He was almost captured many times. Once he had to hide in the woods for a week, eating whatever he could find."

"Let me see. Are there pictures?" asked Kenny.

I grinned to myself. He was hooked like a largemouth bass.

"Here," I said. "There are some words in the stories you might not know. I've made you a vocabulary list."

He glanced at it. "What do they mean?"

I pushed another book over to him. "This is a junior dictionary. If you know the alphabet, you know how to look up words. For example, look up 'gangrene.'"

He did. His eyes lit up. "Cool!"

"I want you to read as much as you can, all the time," I said. "The more you read, the better you'll do in school. Now let's look at today's homework. It's all about context clues."

That evening I skipped into the kitchen and plunked myself down at the table. I was starving. It's hard work, tutoring a beast.

"Today I actually had Kenny sounding out words," I said proudly as Mom passed me the platter of mushroom-shrimp-and-black-olive ravioli.

"I think it's really nice of you to help Kenny out like this," said my dad. "It's funny, but every once in a while his parents and I worry that you two don't like each other."

I waved my hand airily. "Oh, we've come to an understanding," I said.

"I wish we could come to an understanding about your household chores," said my mom, looking unhappy.

I quit chewing. Now what?

"I had asked you to put the wet clothes into the dryer when you came home this afternoon," Mom reminded me. "It would have saved me a lot of time. But you forgot. Again."

I felt bad. I looked through the kitchen door into our laundry area. Three mounds of dirty clothes were waiting to be washed.

My dad frowned over his glasses. "It certainly seems as if you've been forgetting quite a few things lately. Why is that?"

"I have a lot of stuff going on," I said lamely. "I'm tutoring Kenny, I'm in the middle of a great book . . ."

My parents looked at me solemnly. They're usually very easygoing and understanding. I didn't want to let them down.

"I'm sorry," I said. "I'll try to do better."

"Thank you," said Mom.

I sighed to myself as Dad put some vegetables on my plate. I was fixing Kenny's problem, I was saving the Disney Girls from total disaster—why couldn't I handle my own life?

Chapter Fourteen

Thank You, Disney Girls!

I tutored Kenny the whole next week. Guess what. He finished the American Revolution stories and asked me to pick him out something else! I chose one of my favorite science-fiction books. I hoped Kenny would keep reading, even after his school grades improved. I felt good about helping him, even if I was doing it for my own reasons. I had showed him that he could read a lot more things than he had thought—as long as he took his time, sounded out words, looked up words he didn't know, and used his context clues.

By the time we took our test the next Thursday, I

thought he was about as ready as he'd ever be. Afterward, I glanced over at him. He shrugged and looked a little unsure. Had he messed up? If he didn't make at least a C, I wouldn't get the tape back. All my hard work would be for nothing!

Beneath my desk, I held my tiny magic mirror charm, and whispered:

All the magic powers that be,
Hear me now, my special plea.
The Beast and I both tried our best,
Please help him pass his reading test.

There, I thought. Not only had we both worked hard, but we had magic on our side. I felt a little better.

"So are you ever going to tell us what spell you put on Kenny?" Jasmine asked me during art class on Thursday afternoon.

Ella edged closer to me to hear. I grinned mysteriously, trying to seem confident.

"No spell," I said airily. "I have to warn you, though.

The Beast can be tamed for only a short period of time. The last few weeks have been nice, but I can't promise it'll last forever."

Yukiko sighed. "I just wish he would give back that stupid tape," she said. "Even though he hasn't threatened us with it lately—still, it's hanging over our heads."

"I know," I said truthfully. And until we got our tests back on Friday, I would be holding my breath.

"Paula, good work," said Mr. Murchison, handing her back her test. Paula smiled and tilted her paper to show me the A-minus.

I smiled. My knees felt like jelly.

"Aaron, brush up on your homonyms, okay?" said our teacher.

"Okay," said Aaron, reading his grade.

"Alicia, good," continued Mr. Murchison, handing out papers. "Samantha, not your best work, I'm afraid. Michael, you can do better, too."

He handed me mine. "Excellent, as usual, Isabelle."

Please, let Kenny have earned a C or better, I pleaded silently.

"Kenny," said Mr. Murchison. "I was very pleased with this. You've obviously been working hard. Good for you."

Kenny read his grade and looked surprised and happy. He knew I was staring at him, so he placed his test faceup on his desk. By leaning over a little and craning my neck, I could read his grade. He had gotten a B! He hadn't needed my magic after all! Just my help.

I breathed an enormous sigh of relief.

After lunch I raced to my cubby. There it was, sticking out of my backpack. One videocassette. Its label said, "Isabelle's Greatest Hits. Rated H, for Hilarious, and S, for Stupid."

I didn't care what Kenny had rated it. He had held up his end of our deal. I couldn't wait to tell my friends!

On Saturday the Disney Girls had a sleepover. No, not at my house. I'll probably be forty-five years old before I host another sleepover at my house! This time we all met at Paula's.

I like Paula's house. Our houses are a little bit the same, because they're both very small. The rooms are even arranged the same way inside. But our house is very uncluttered and modern, with white walls, simple furniture, and lots of African art.

The Pintos' house is full of . . . stuff. There are stacks of books everywhere, mostly about engineering or veterinary medicine. Paula's dad is an engineer. He designs bridges and things like that. So there are small models of bridges and dams balanced on top of the books. Mrs. Pinto is going back to school to be a veterinarian. Crammed in next to the model bridges are models of a horse's insides, or a dog's ear. Paula wants to be a vet, too, when she grows up. Which is a good thing, because the Pintos have more pets than anyone else I know.

They have two greyhounds, who used to be racing dogs. Their names are Duchess and Jazzhot. The Pintos rescued them when they were retired from the dog track. Then there's a beagle named Bobby. Bobby has only three legs, but he can run very fast and jump up on the couches and stuff. Paula also has three cats. Mr. Pinto named them Stopit, Getdown, and Nomore. They came from the Orlando Animal Shelter.

But Paula's personal pet is a real live raccoon, named (of

course) Meeko. Mostly he's supposed to stay out on their screened porch, but Paula almost always sneaks him inside. He makes the dogs and cats crazy.

Everywhere you look are leashes, dog brushes, cat brushes, pet vitamins, and other pet-care stuff, all piled next to the books and the different models.

Tonight my mom dropped me off at Paula's house right at five o'clock. The tape was burning a hole in my backpack, but I waited until all six of us were together.

Then I said, "Before we have dinner, I want to give you all a present. But you can't ask me how I got it. Okay?"

"Okay," they chorused, looking curious.

I whipped the tape out. Ella gasped and put her hand over her mouth. Ariel shrieked and grabbed it out of my hand. Paula smiled and shook her head wonderingly. Jasmine stared at me thoughtfully. Yukiko jumped up and started dancing around.

I sat back and grinned.

"How did you—" Jasmine began, but I held up my hand.

"Sorry. Sworn to secrecy. But let's just thank our magic stars," I said.

After everyone had recovered from the excitement of

the tape, Jasmine coughed into her hand.

"Ahem," she said. "Thank you very much for the tape, no matter how you got it. But we all have a present for you, too."

"For me?" I asked, confused. "Why?"

My five friends looked at each other.

"We couldn't help noticing that you've been having some problems at home," Jasmine said. "You know, forgetting to do stuff, your mom getting on your case. So we decided to try to help you."

Yukiko reached into her overnight bag and handed me an envelope. Inside were a bunch of strips of heavy paper.

I looked at them. They were an inch wide and six inches long. My friends had decorated them with glitter and stickers and gold, sparkly ink. On each one was written something like, "Feed Snuffles and Pokey." Or "Empty your waste basket." Or "Put newspapers in the recycling bin."

"They're great," I said. "But what are they?"

Jasmine laughed. "They're bookmarks! See, you'll put them into whatever book you're reading, every ten or fifteen pages. Then when you come to it, it'll remind you to do whatever it says."

"Or it'll remind you that you need to do *something*," said Yukiko. "Even if it's not that exact thing. It was Jasmine's idea."

"Ohhh, I get it—that's terrific," I said, getting excited. I pulled out *Once More the King* (I was almost finished) and counted off pages. "Guys, this is fantastic! I will never, ever forget another thing! Why didn't I think of this ages ago? My folks are going to be so happy!"

I meant it. I thought it was a brilliant idea. I gazed at my best friends. They had put a lot of thought into this, into helping me. "You guys are great," I said.

They laughed. "What are friends for?" asked Jasmine.

"And now, starring in their very own video," intoned Paula, popping our tape into the VCR. "The . . . Disney Girls!"

It was late. Our sleepover was winding down. But we had saved the best for last. And here it was: a videotape of my family room, as seen through our basement window. Sometimes the video was out of focus, and you actually couldn't hear us that well, which made it worse, because you didn't know why we were dancing around like lunatics.

I cringed when I saw myself clutching my dad's golf club, obviously singing. Jasmine giggled. Then we saw Paula doing her theme song, and we all giggled harder. Kenny hadn't gotten all of us on tape, but he'd been right about one thing: it *was* rated H, for Hilarious.

Soon the six of us were laughing so hard we had to lie down on our sleeping bags. As I lay there, gasping for breath, I remembered wondering why I couldn't seem to fix my own problems. Now I realized why: because I had four best friends now, and one *best* best friend. And I could rely on them to help me.

"Thank you, magic powers that be," I whispered. "Thank you very much."

"Listen, you guys," I said. "We're going to do an art project for the new baby. We have a big, confusing family, and the baby will need all the help it can get. We're going to make a photo album of our family."

I made my frame pink, and scalloped the edges. I wrote my name in fancy curlicue letters. Then I put flower and heart stickers all over it. Next I cut out a white frame for the baby. I handed it around to my brothers so they could each add a decoration.

I had almost finished Mom's frame when the baby's frame got back to me. I stared at it in horror. Each one of the Dwarfs had decorated it for a *boy*. There were football stickers, race cars, trucks, and male action figures.

"You guys," I cried, "what if the baby is a girl?"

My brothers stared at me silently for a moment. Then they burst into laughter.

"A *girl*?" asked Michael. He sneezed. "It won't be a girl."

"Mom and Dad wouldn't know what to do with a girl," said Yoshi. He glanced at me quickly and said, "A *baby* girl, that is."

"Of course it's going to be another boy," said Ben confidently.

"The. New. Baby. Will. Be. A. Girl," I said through gritted teeth. "Get. Used. To. It."

Read all of the books in the
Disney Girls series!

#1 One of Us

Jasmine is thrilled to be a Disney Girl. It means she has four best friends—Ariel, Yukiko, Paula, and Ella. But she still doesn't have a *best,* best friend. Then she meets Isabelle Beaumont, the new girl. Maybe Isabelle could be Jasmine's best best friend—but could she be a *Disney Girl*?

#2 Attack of the Beast: Isabelle's Story

Isabelle's next-door neighbor Kenny has been a total Beast for as long as she can remember. But now he's gone too far: he secretly videotaped the Disney Girls singing and dancing and acting silly at Isabelle's slumber party. Isabelle vows to get the tape back, but how will she ever get past the Beast?

#3 And Sleepy Makes Seven

Mrs. Hayashi is expecting a baby soon, and Yukiko is praying that this time it'll be a girl. She's already got six younger brothers and stepbrothers, and this is her last chance for a sister. All of the Disney Girls are hoping that with a little magic, Yukiko's fondest wish will come true.

#4 A Fish out of Water

Ariel in ballet class? That's like putting a fish in the middle of the desert! Even though Ariel's the star of her swim team, she decides that she wants to spend more time with the other Disney Girls. So she joins Jasmine and Yukiko's ballet class. But has Ariel made a mistake, or will she trade in her flippers for toe shoes forever?

#5 *Cinderella's Castle*

The Disney Girls are so excited about the school's holiday party. Ella decides that the perfect thing for her to make is an elaborate gingerbread castle. But creating such a complicated confection isn't easy, even for someone as superorganized as Ella. And her stepfamily just doesn't seem to understand how important this is to her. Ella could really use a fairy godmother right now . . .

#6 *One Pet Too Many*

Paula's always loved animals, any animal. Who else would have a pet raccoon, not to mention two cats, a dog, three rabbits, and countless fish? When Paula finds a lost baby armadillo, though, her parents say, "No more pets!"—and that's that. But how much trouble could a baby armadillo be? Plenty, as Paula discovers—especially when she's trying to keep it a secret from her parents.

#7 *Adventure in Walt Disney World:*
 A Disney Girls Super Special

The Disney Girls are so excited. They're all going to dress up as their favorite Disney Princesses and participate in the Magic Kingdom Princess Parade. And as a special treat, Jasmine's mom is taking them to stay overnight at a hotel in the park. Magical things are bound to happen to the Disney Girls in the most magical place on earth—and they do . . .